Freedom Knows No Color

by
Anne Schraff

Perfection Learning® Corporation
Logan, Iowa 51546

Cover Illustration: Doug Knutson
Cover Design: Deborah Lea Bell
Michael A. Aspengren

For information, contact
Perfection Learning® Corporation
1000 North Second Avenue, P.O. Box 500
Logan, Iowa 51546-1099.
Tel: 1-800-831-4190 • Fax: 1-712-644-2392
Paperback ISBN 0-7891-5136-7
Cover Craft® ISBN 0-7807-9270-x
Printed in the U.S.A.
5 6 7 8 9 10 PP 09 08 07 06 05 04

1   Old Ed Whitney lay dying in the parlor of the big house. His voice was weak as he talked to his wife. "Abigail, you're not to sell my slaves to that brother of yours. Do you hear me? Not Julian, nor any of them. I know you're of a mind to do it. But for the love of God, don't!"

Julian Holland had just turned 18 in this winter of 1858. Now he hid in the shadow of an oak tree just outside the parlor window. He strained his ears to hear the benign old man's last words.

"Just be quiet, Edward. Save your strength," Abigail Whitney said in a flat, dry voice. She was as cruel a woman as her husband was kind.

Julian had lived on the Whitneys' farm in Louisiana all his life. He took care of the hogs, did farm chores, and helped at the house when needed. Julian and the other slaves had always been treated with kindness by the old man. But Mrs. Whitney hated them all. And she hated Julian in particular.

Now the old woman left her dying husband's bedside and opened the

Proche de la maison

back door of the big house. "You're sneaking around out here, aren't you, Julian?" she called in a low, sly voice. "I know you're out there listening. I know it very well. So I'll give you something to think about. The old man won't last till morning. Then you and the rest of your black friends are going north to Mister Cannon's cotton plantation." She let out a crackling laugh. "Oh yes, indeed. I won't have to look at your lazy faces anymore, and you'll work to the music of a lash!"

Still laughing, Mrs. Whitney closed the door, and Julian quietly left the shelter of the oak. He returned to the slave quarters, a few log cabins some distance from the house. Julian's three companions waited eagerly for news. They had all lived here many years and were used to Master Whitney's kind treatment. They were provided with decent food on a regular basis and comfortable living conditions. All of Master Whitney's slaves slept on straw beds, and the walls of the cabins were tight against the rain.

Où veut habiter

"It's true," Julian said sadly. "If Master Ed dies, we'll be sent north to the Cannon plantation. We'll be field hands."

Thomas, a tall, lanky 20-year-old, muttered, "I won't go. I'll run away, go south to New Orleans."

"They'll catch you and whip you half to death," 17-year-old Daniel warned. "You don't stand a chance."

"It's better than being shipped off to the Cannon plantation," Thomas advised. "You should come too."

"I'm too old to run," Uncle Jeb said. Jebediah Samson was 70. "I'm too near to crossing over that last river. Besides, I don't think Master Cannon will want me. I wouldn't be much use as a field hand."

Julian said nothing, but he envied Thomas's daring. It was different though with Thomas than with the others. He'd been free once. Thomas had been kidnapped from the docks of New Orleans and forced into slavery at the age of 15. Julian had never been free. He didn't know what freedom was. The only life he knew was as a slave on the Whitney farm.

Julian had vague memories of his mother. She was darkly beautiful and would cradle him in her arms and sing him lullabies. But she had died long ago. After her death, Ed Whitney looked out for Julian. He would bring him trinkets to play with, a little carved wooden horse, a spinning toy. He made sure that Julian had shoes in the wet Louisiana winters, and in the summer he would often take the boy fishing. Mr. Whitney favored the orphaned boy over all the others. Julian never knew why, but the old man's kindness was welcome.

And now Ed Whitney, Julian's protector, was dying. The peaceful days of tending the hogs and cutting wood and going fishing would soon be gone.

At midnight, the piercing scream of Aunt Sally announced the death of the Master. Aunt Sally and Uncle Jeb had taken care of the Whitney household for over 30 years. Now the black woman howled with genuine anguish, for she had deep affection for the kind old man. In the last few days, it had been Aunt Sally who had cooled the old man's brow with wet rags. Abigail Whitney had gone about her work of keeping the books, dry-eyed and expressionless.

Thomas set out through the darkness at once. He hoped to make it through the tangled cypress woods and over the bayous to New Orleans. Clouds had rolled over the moon and now covered his escape. Standing outside the log cabins, Julian and Daniel sadly watched him go.

Daniel's eyes filled with fear as Thomas disappeared into the woods. "I'm scared, Julian," he admitted. "I'm scared to run, and I'm scared to stay. Remember last summer when we heard the bloodhounds baying, and everybody said they were running down slaves? Remember when we saw that black man floating in the bayou the next morning?"

Julian nodded. "Likely he was shot running away."

"Julian, what do you know about the Cannon plantation?" Daniel asked.

"Seems like it must be a real hard place, Daniel," Julian replied. "Missus is always bragging about how tough her brother is, how he makes everybody work so hard. She claims he's broken more slaves than any man in Louisiana."

"Working on a plantation is killing work," Daniel said, shaking his head. "It won't be like working here."

Julian stared toward the big house where the Whitneys lived. It didn't have the grandeur of some of the other mansions in the bayou country. It didn't have great balconies and long stairways, or fountains with statues hidden among the roses and vines. But it was still a beautiful house. And even though Julian didn't live there, he thought of it as home.

When he was very small, Julian had played on the porch with Howard Whitney, Mr. Whitney's son. Howard was a friendly, red-haired boy who had shared his toys with Julian. Howard and Julian had grown up together like brothers, riding horses, swinging from the trees, and playing boys' games. Now Howard was away at school, and Mr. Whitney was dead. And Julian had no allies left.

Julian felt the sort of grief a boy would feel at the death of a grandfather. He had tried to go to Mr. Whitney in his last days and offer a word of comfort to him. But Mrs. Whitney had always barred the way.

"He has no need of slaves troubling him," she had snapped when Julian made the request.

"Missus," Julian had said politely, "your husband has been real kind to me. I'd just like to pay my respects."

"Away with you!" Mrs. Whitney had said in a harsh voice. "You just want to get into the house and steal something. You're all thieves. You just want to snatch something, figuring he's too sick to notice."

"No, ma'am, I'd never steal from Master Whitney," Julian said, deeply hurt.

"Liar!" Mrs. Whitney cried. "I'm no fool like my husband. I can see right through the bunch of you. You'd steal the bed right out from under him if you thought you could get away with it. Now away with you, and stop troubling me."

So Julian never got to say good-bye to Mr. Whitney. And now he was dead.

The next day Julian watched as friends and relatives arrived at the big house. In all the excitement, Mrs. Whitney had not yet noticed that Thomas was gone. Julian and Daniel did the chores Thomas usually performed so he would not be missed any sooner than necessary. They wanted to give him a head start on the slave catchers who would pursue him—the men called *patterollers*.

Howard Whitney, Julian's childhood companion, arrived in a fine carriage. As he headed toward the house, he never even looked in the direction of the slave quarters. Julian called a soft "Hello, Master Howard" as the young man passed, but he didn't seem to hear it. Or maybe he didn't want to hear it. It was acceptable for black and white children to play together when they were young. But the friendships always ended when they became teenagers.

At the burial of Mr. Whitney, the slaves stood respectfully at the edge of the graveyard listening to the preacher praise his good qualities. Mrs. Whitney had stood by impassively, never shedding a tear. Howard Whitney looked very sad.

Afterward as Howard was leaving, Julian called to him again.

"Master Howard," Julian said.

"Oh, hello, Julian," Howard said, standing by the carriage that would take him back to school.

"I'm sorry about your father. He was a fine man," Julian said.

"Thank you, Julian. He thought highly of you," Howard said, reaching for the door handle on the carriage. He seemed eager to be on his way.

Suddenly Julian's mind was filled with the times he and Howard had shared as children. Julian felt a deep dread at the thought of leaving the Whitney place and going to the Cannon plantation. Maybe Master Howard could do something, he thought. Maybe he could change Abigail Whitney's mind. "Missus is shipping us to her brother's cotton plantation by the Red River," Julian began.

A look of pain crossed Howard's handsome face. "Uncle Cyrus's plantation," he said. "Yes, well, my mother is not keeping this place. She's selling off all the stock, and she has no need of slaves."

"Master Howard, I've heard tales of that place," Julian said as respectfully as he could.

"Uncle Cyrus is a stern man, Julian, but I'm sure he's not cruel," Howard said. He looked uncomfortable. He turned then, climbed into the carriage, and was gone.

It's not his fault, Julian thought sadly. He's only a boy himself.

Two days later, Mr. Horton, the overseer from the Cannon plantation, came to the Whitney farm. He brought two burly slaves with him. Horton had the names of all of Ed Whitney's slaves written on a piece of paper, and he stood reading them off.

"Daniel Jackson, age 17," he began. "Julian Holland, age 18. Thomas Crawford, age 20. Jeb Samson, age 70."

Aunt Sally was standing nearby, and she let out a cry of anguish. "Not Jeb, Missus," she begged Abigail Whitney. "Jeb's not fit for field work. Please don't send Jeb away." Uncle Jeb had been with the Whitneys for as long as Aunt Sally had. And while the two were never allowed to marry, they had always loved each other.

"Be quiet and go into the house," Mrs. Whitney scolded.

Weeping, Aunt Sally obeyed.

The overseer's flinty eyes found Julian, Daniel, and Jeb, but Thomas was missing. "Where's Thomas Crawford?" he asked.

No one answered.

"You heard the man," Mrs. Whitney

shouted. "Where's Thomas?"

"He was missing this morning, Missus," Julian said. "Don't know what's become of him."

Mrs. Whitney glared at the three slaves. Then she seized on the one who was the weakest and most likely to betray Thomas. "Uncle Jeb, you know where Thomas has gone, don't you?" she demanded. "Would you like a whipping, Jeb, or are you going to tell me the truth?"

"Missus, I'm so tired when I lay me down at night, I never hear or see anything," Jeb answered.

Suddenly Horton produced a heavy cowhide whip.

"You'll all be beaten unless someone tells me where Thomas is," Mrs. Whitney threatened.

The overseer cracked his whip against a tree, peeling away a strip of bark as a warning. His thick-muscled arms tightened, ready to deliver the lashes.

2 Abigail Whitney stepped forward and said to the overseer, "Never mind, Mr. Horton. I don't want them going to my brother damaged. The scamp will be caught. He can't have gone far. Tell my brother I'll send him when we catch him."

The old woman turned to Julian then and said, "You need not look smug. I'll have the last laugh! I've sent word to my brother that you're rebellious and will need severe treatment to break your wicked spirit. You might have been Edward's pet, but you'll be Cyrus's whipping boy! That I know for sure!"

Julian climbed onto the wagon with Daniel and Uncle Jeb. He fought back tears as he watched the only home he'd ever known disappear from sight. He had never understood why Mrs. Whitney despised him so. Through the years, Mr. Whitney had always managed to spare Julian from her wrath. That had been enough to make his life relatively happy. But now the old woman was sending him north, into an unknown that Julian feared with all his heart.

The wagon rumbled through the cypress and tupelo swamps, then past the freshwater swamps. Finally it reached the valley of the Red River where cotton was grown.

The next day, they reached the Cannon plantation. Julian and the others were immediately taken to the big log house that served as the slave quarters. The house was a far cry from the snug little cabins at the Whitney farm. Julian noticed big cracks between the logs. He knew that when it rained, life would be miserable within those walls.

A slave named Nat showed them where they would sleep.

"We sleep on wooden planks?" Daniel asked in dismay.

"Well, we used to bring in moss to make it softer," Nat said, "but then the fleas came. We couldn't get any rest for the fleas eating us alive."

Julian thought longingly of the

comfortable beds at the Whitney farm.

"What do you get to eat here?" Daniel asked.

"Corn and bacon," Nat replied. "Every Sunday morning we get enough corn to make a peck of meal. And we get three and a half pounds of bacon. We have to make it last all week, 'cause there's no more till Sunday comes again."

Julian listened numbly to the details. He had not yet met Cyrus Cannon, but he was already desperate. He wished he had gone with Thomas. Whatever happened couldn't have been worse than this beastly existence.

That night Julian couldn't sleep. He rolled from side to side on the wooden plank trying to find a comfortable position.

In the darkness, Nat whispered, "Don't worry, boy. Once the work starts, you'll be so tired you'll be able to sleep on nails!"

Julian sighed and thought about the times he had gone fishing with Ed Whitney. Julian and Howard and some of the other boys would rise before dawn. They'd all pile into a wagon, and Mr. Whitney would take them to a nearby river. There they'd pull catfish and bullheads out of the water and fry them over an open fire. When they grew tired of fishing, they'd strip off their clothes and dive into the river, splashing and roughhousing.

It hadn't seemed much like slavery then. It was his life, and he accepted it. He couldn't remember ever longing for freedom the way he did now. But since Mr. Whitney had died, it seemed that's all he thought of.

An anger stirred within Julian. The injustice of what had happened to him and Daniel and Uncle Jeb rankled him like a raw wound. He remembered Aunt Sally pleading for Uncle Jeb. Now the two were torn apart and would probably never see each other again. How could anyone sell human beings like chickens and hogs? he wondered bitterly.

Julian had still not slept when the horn sounded, signaling the start of a new day. There was a mad scramble to make breakfast and to fill gourds with water for use during the day. Then to fill another gourd with corn meal cake and bacon for the midday meal. If you didn't get it all done quickly, you'd go into the fields unprepared.

"Hurry along," Nat advised Julian. "You get caught here in the quarters after daybreak, you'll get a flogging."

Julian ate his cornmeal cake and rushed into the fields with the others. Daniel had hurried out with him, but Uncle Jeb was nowhere in sight. At first Julian worried, but then he reasoned that Uncle Jeb was an old man. They knew he would probably not be able to keep up. They must have found something else for him to do.

It was March, and the ground was all prepared for the cotton crop. The mules had plowed six-foot-wide beds. Now a mule pulled the plow down the center of each bed, drilling holes. The women had sacks of cottonseed around their necks, and they dropped a seed in each hole. Another mule followed with a harrow to cover the seed. Julian soon saw that it took two mules and three slaves to plant a row of cotton.

Julian had worked with mules before and was glad when he was given the job of running a plow. At first he was able to keep up with the others. Within a few hours, however, he was exhausted by the fast pace of the work. He wasn't used to it. He breathed a deep sigh of relief when it was finally lunchtime. But he couldn't believe it when Mr. Horton shouted, "You've got 10 minutes to eat. No more than that. No lagging now."

Ten minutes? At the Whitney farm, they were always given half an hour, sometimes more.

Julian wolfed down his meal. He felt like one of the mules, driven to endless toil, working until it dropped. He had never been so tired.

In the days that followed, the work only got worse. The cotton plants appeared in little more than a week.

Now the slaves labored down the rows, hoeing out the weeds.

It was when the hoeing started that Julian finally met Cyrus Cannon. Cannon was a huge man whose muscles seemed to strain against his clothes and high boots. His face was lined deep from the sun, and he had large, crooked teeth and pitiless eyes. He wore his blonde hair long, and a straggly beard hung from his chin like Spanish moss.

Now Cannon sat astride a nervous bay horse and sized up the slaves. His gaze went from slave to slave, as if he could measure the worth of each by a single look. His hard stare landed on Julian. "You'd be Julian from my sister's farm," he said.

"Yessir, Master Cannon," Julian said immediately, never meeting the other man's eyes.

A sneer touched the man's thin lips as he pulled out a whip. "You look pretty fast to me, Julian. I want you to take the lead row."

Frightened, Julian walked to the

lead row and began working as fast as he could.

During the hoeing, overseers on horseback rode behind the slaves, whipping those who lagged behind. Mr. Cannon took that role himself now, riding behind Julian as Julian wielded the hoe. Julian thought he was moving fast, but it was not fast enough for Cannon. The sting of the whip suddenly jolted Julian's body.

Julian had never felt the whip before. The shock was almost worse than the pain. He stumbled, then righted himself and began hoeing at a frantic pace.

"You are one slow darky," Cannon yelled.

Again the whip fell, goading Julian on. The faster he went, the closer Cannon came to him. Julian could feel the hot breath of the horse on his neck. Cannon cursed Julian and cried, "Faster, boy!"

At the end of the row, Cannon's big horse wheeled. "Well," Cannon said, "you're not as balky as Abigail let on.

You'll make a fine field hand when I get done with you."

Julian felt a rush of hatred that shocked him with its power. At that minute he could easily have dragged Cyrus Cannon from his horse and hurled him into the river. Julian had never felt such hatred. He had disliked Mrs. Whitney, but Mr. Whitney had always stood between Julian and the woman's hostility. Now it was only Julian and Cyrus Cannon. Cannon, sneering through his crooked teeth, wielding the whip with glee. Cannon, like a kind of devil arisen from the flames of hell. And there was nobody, nothing to stop him.

The slaves finally dragged themselves back to the quarters at sundown. But there were still the regular chores to do. It was Julian's job to chop wood for the cabin for the next day. With his muscles aching and his back still sore from the whip, he cut a load of wood. Then he carried as much as he could back to the log house. There he found Daniel grinding corn in a hand mill for the next day's meal. Nat was sitting beside him repairing a hoe handle.

"The real work starts when the cotton comes up," Nat warned as he worked. "Then's the time you work so hard you think you're going to die. No, you're *sure* you're going to die. They lash you hard the first day so you pick a whole lot of cotton. That's how they know how much you can really do. And every day after, they weigh what you pick. And it better not be less than what you picked that first day, or you get whipped for lagging behind."

Julian made a final trip to the woodpile in the moonlight to get another armload of wood. That was when he saw the man lying against a fence. Julian looked hard and made out Jeb. His back was against the post, and his legs were stretched out before him on the ground.

"Jeb, what are you doing over there?" Julian asked, heading toward the old man.

"They put me to cutting wood all

day, Julian," Uncle Jeb said, grimacing and clutching his hand to his heart. "Then they sent me out again after dinner. But this time my legs done quit on me. I got so tired I just couldn't move. And I got this powerful pain going through me now. I thought if I sat awhile, it'd pass, but it hasn't."

"Jeb, what can I do for you?" Julian asked.

"I don't figure there's much you can do, Julian," Jeb said. "I expect my heart is quitting on me. I've been a slave a long time, boy. Before I came to the Whitney farm, I worked a big plantation, and it was hard, hard work. I'm worn out now, boy."

"Jeb, how can I help you?" Julian wanted to know. "You've always been so good to me."

Uncle Jeb breathed hard. Then he said, "Boy, there's one way you can help me."

"How?" Julian asked anxiously. The old man seemed to be fading fast. "Just tell me what it is."

"When I go, you make sure they

dress me in my best clothes," Uncle Jeb began. "I got a dark suit in among my things. It's not a fancy suit, but it's the best I got." He paused for a moment, trying to control his raspy breathing. Then he continued. "And I know there won't be no preacher saying words over me, so if you'd say some words . . ."

"What do you want me to say, Jeb?" Julian said.

"Just say 'Lord, take Jeb Samson to the gates of glory, and let him rest there in Heaven.' "

Julian nodded. "I'll do that, Jeb," he said sadly. He could feel his eyes filling up with tears. "I'll see that you're dressed in your best suit, and I'll say those words."

The old man's trembling hand found Julian's then and grasped it. "Listen close now, boy. Tomorrow at this time I'll be gone. Nothing more anybody can do to these old bones. But some time if you want to make a run for it, if you want to take your chances . . ." He began to cough then.

It was a full minute before he could go on.

"Listen now," Jeb said. Julian leaned closer. "Follow the river. Don't ever lose sight of the river. If you're going south to New Orleans, in about a night's walk you'll see a house—a big white house with oak trees and a big rooster weather vane on the roof. A white man lives there who's against slavery. They say he's crazy. He has wild gray hair and a long, scraggly beard. Always wears a long black coat. But he's what they call an abolitionist. He'll help you, boy. You understand?"

Julian frowned. What was Uncle Jeb mumbling about? A white man who didn't like slavery? An abolitionist? Julian had never heard that word before.

He paid little attention to what the old man said. All he could think of was that Uncle Jeb, his friend for all his life, was sitting propped up against a fence post dying outdoors like a dog. A man should die in bed, in his own home, surrounded by people who loved him.

"Jeb, can I fetch a doctor?" Julian said.

Jeb shook his head and sighed, "I'm a goner, boy. But I wish you'd sing me a saving song before I go."

Julian shook his head. "I don't know any saving songs."

Jeb was breathing in a shallow way now. "Sing 'Steal away, steal away to Jesus, Steal away, steal away home . . .' You know that one. Aunt Sally used to sing it while she worked in the kitchen."

Julian remembered. He leaned close to Jeb and sang the saving hymn. As he sang, he put his arm around Jeb and let the old man's head lie against his chest. He was holding Uncle Jeb in his arms that way when a seizure wrenched Jeb's body. Then a surprised look came to Jeb's face. A trickle of saliva ran down his chin. His eyes closed, and his chest ceased moving. And Julian knew that he was dead.

3 As the summer wore on, the days grew hotter and more miserable. Heat seemed to rise from the cotton fields like steam from a kettle.

"Sometimes I wish I'd gone like Uncle Jeb did—right away after we got here," Daniel groaned. The cotton was a foot high now. The fields had to be hoed again before the cotton picking season started in August. "Every time I lay me down at night, Julian, I hope I don't wake up in the morning. I'm so miserable I wish I was dead."

Julian knew how Daniel felt. But he had been thinking about what Uncle Jeb had told him before he died. About the man who would help them if they tried to escape. Maybe there was some truth to what Jeb had said.

"It won't always be like this, Daniel," Julian said. "Maybe one of these days we'll do what Thomas did. He must have made it. They never brought him here, so he must have gotten through. He's probably in New Orleans now, living good."

Daniel shook his head. "They got Thomas. They killed him. I feel it in my bones that they killed him. He never made it to New Orleans. He's out in some swamp somewhere with the crocodiles chewing on his bones."

"Listen, Daniel," Julian said. "I heard from Uncle Jeb that there are folks who will help us, white folks . . ."

Daniel looked at Julian as if he were crazy. "There's no such thing," he said.

"Abolitionists are what they call themselves, Daniel," Julian explained. "They don't like slavery, and they help runaway slaves. That's what Uncle Jeb said."

Daniel shook his head. "Never heard such nonsense in my life. Why would a white man care about slavery? No white man that I know of has ever been a slave."

"Just keep up your spirits, Daniel," Julian said. "Our time's coming. We just have to be patient."

"Our time's never going to come," Daniel said, his shoulders drooping.

Most days now Cyrus Cannon was

in the fields, following the slaves on his bay horse. He used his whip ruthlessly. It landed on Daniel's shoulders more often than on Julian's. Julian was a better hoer than Daniel even when the younger boy was doing his best to keep up. Cannon seemed to be singling him out for punishment. Daniel looked confused and desperate as the whip struck him again and again.

Julian could stand it no longer. He pleaded for his friend. "He doesn't mean to go so slow, Master Cannon. He'll get faster if you give him the chance."

Anger narrowed Cannon's eyes, making them slits in his ruddy face. "I don't need advice from slaves," he said. "You're forgetting your place, boy, just like Abigail said you would. Horton! Take him out of the row!"

Horton removed Julian from the row and automatically marched him over to a gum tree. He had obviously done this before. He stripped off Julian's shirt and then tied his wrists to a low-hanging branch. Then Cyrus Cannon came over carrying the whip that he never seemed to be without. "I think your little remarks are worth 25 of these," he said, smacking the thick handle against his hand.

"One!" he yelled as he slashed at Julian with the whip. Blood ran down Julian's back, and welts the size of a little finger rose up on his skin. Julian had never felt such pain. He was afraid he would die before Cannon stopped. He knew men had been whipped to death before. But he clung to the hope that he would survive. Cyrus Cannon wouldn't want to kill a valuable young slave, especially with the picking season just ahead.

"Twenty-five!" Cannon lowered the whip and approached Julian. "Don't you *ever* tell me how to treat my slaves," he screamed into Julian's face. Spit flew from Cannon's angry mouth, spattering Julian's cheeks. "You don't tell a white man *anything*, do you hear? 'Yes, Master' and 'no, Master' is all I ever want to hear you say. *Do you understand?"*

Julian was stunned almost speechless by the pain. "Yes, Master," he managed to say. In a few minutes, bleeding back and all, he was back in the row, hoeing with the others.

For the next few weeks, every day was the same. Julian got up before the sun and didn't finish until the sun went down. Sometimes he didn't even finish then. On nights when the moon was full, the slaves worked in the fields until midnight. Then they did their evening chores by candlelight.

In August as harvesttime approached, a kind of frenzy took over the plantation. Julian didn't know what to expect because he'd never harvested cotton before.

"You won't be plucking pecans from trees like you did at that farm where you were," Nat warned the night before picking began. "You've never seen anything like this, boy."

The next morning, Julian stood in line with the other slaves while a sack was put around his neck. A strap held the sack open. The open mouth of the sack was chest-high, leaving the picker's hands free to pull cotton.

"You're going to work faster than you've ever worked before," Nat whispered from behind Julian in line. "And then you're going to work faster still."

Julian whispered back to Nat, "What if you don't pick as much as you can? Then they won't expect so much from you tomorrow and the next day."

Nat sneered. "Every slave is expected to pick about 200 pounds. They know that, Julian. Don't ever come short of that, or you'll get the whip again. We're all tasked according to how good we are, but nobody's allowed to pick less than 200 pounds."

Julian started up his row in the blazing August sun. Wide-branched trees shaded the plantation house. But the trees in the cotton fields had been cleared years before. There was nothing above the workers but the searing sun.

Cyrus Cannon wore his wide-brimmed hat and rode his bay horse, charging up and down the rows like a madman. He didn't seem to mind the perspiration streaming down his face. He didn't care that his shirt was stuck to him. He looked like a man driven by a desperate cause. His one purpose in life was to make sure that every slave worked as hard as possible. Cannon wielded his whip at anybody who stopped for even a minute.

"Faster!" he screamed at Julian. "You lazy, good-for-nothing black mule. Faster, I tell you! I know you're holding back. You fill those baskets at the row's end, or you'll feel this cowhide like you never felt it before."

Julian thought the day would never end. He was certain his legs would give out or he'd drop from heatstroke. In the 10 minutes allowed for lunch, he guzzled water from his gourd and barely touched the bacon. He needed the water more than food. He thought he could drink up a river if given the chance. And he welcomed the wooden plank waiting for him at the end of the day.

Back in the rows, he forced his mind back to the Whitney farm. On a hot day like today, Ed Whitney, Howard, and the slaves would all go down to the river for a swim. They'd holler and splash and ride logs in the cool water. Ed would laugh when Howard reminded him how angry Mrs. Whitney would be over the chores left undone.

"That woman," Ed Whitney would laugh. "She's the bane of my life."

Now, Julian could almost feel the cool river water bathing his weary, hot body. He felt so tired, so hot and dizzy. A slight breeze had come up, and when it blew on Julian's sweat-drenched body, it felt as if he were swimming in his own perspiration.

The cotton grew seven feet high, and each stalk had branches going out in every direction. The branches overlapped one another, making it easy to break one no matter how careful the pickers were. But cotton would not bloom again on a broken branch, and that was a loss to the plantation owner.

Late in the day, Daniel broke a branch. Before he hardly realized what he had done, wild curses flew from Cannon's mouth and the whip met Daniel's back. Julian watched, stunned, as his cowering friend was punished. Julian wanted to do something. Every fiber of his being cried out for him to do something. He felt like grabbing anything that could be used as a weapon and charging at Cyrus Cannon. He imagined the old devil lying as dead and broken as the branch in the furrow.

Julian knew he couldn't stand this much longer. He realized that if he continued this way, he would one day lose control and kill Cannon.

Julian and Daniel continued picking the cotton with the others, filling the baskets from their sacks. Like animals, Julian thought again. It was more true every day. What can a poor, dumb animal do but plod along, suffering, with nothing to hope for? With only death to end its pain?

Horton called a halt to work, and the slaves trekked toward the gin house where the cotton was weighed. Some of the slaves worried that they had picked too little. If so, a flogging awaited them. Julian was too tired and too desperate to care. But when his cotton was weighed, he had picked 250 pounds.

"That's what you'll pick every day from now on," the man in the gin house said. "You must never do less."

Julian carried his ponderous baskets to the cotton house, where the cotton was stored like hay. All the slaves joined in tramping it down to make room for more. Then back at the log cabin, the nightly chores began. Julian went to cut wood and Daniel to feed the hogs. After that, working by candlelight, they would prepare the next day's meal.

But that night Julian decided that he and Daniel would not eat their meal there tomorrow. No breakfast in the slave quarters, no hurried lunch in the cotton fields.

"Tonight," Julian whispered to Daniel as they headed out to do their chores.

Daniel's eyes grew wide, but he nodded. "I trust you, Julian," was all he said.

"Listen for my sign, the saving song," Julian said.

Daniel nodded again.

"Just do your chores as usual," Julian instructed. "We don't want to raise any suspicions." Slaves did not usually betray one another, but Julian was afraid that somebody desperate for some slight advantage might say the wrong thing. Some weary slave who longed to work at the house instead of in the fields might whisper something. Julian didn't want to risk their chances.

Later Julian lay down on the board he slept on, and Daniel did the same. Through a big crack in the opposite wall they could see the moonlight seeping in. But the sky was full of clouds that night. And Julian knew that when the clouds rolled over the moon, the boys had their best chance of fleeing.

Often one or more of the slaves would sing a saving song in the evening. It helped everyone quiet down and fall into sleep. Nobody was surprised when Julian's clear, young voice rose in the log cabin. "Steal away, steal away to Jesus," Julian sang softly over the wild pounding of his heart. "Steal away, steal away home . . ."

The moonlight had disappeared from the crack in the wall. It was time. Julian got up first and Daniel followed.

They headed out of the cabin and silently raced through the darkness. Julian expected a rifle to spit fire at their fleeing backs. He knew they could both be dead by this time tomorrow. Maybe long dead.

But Julian now knew what freedom was. He had never had it, but he sensed what it was, and he wanted it. He wanted it desperately.

Julian wanted freedom more than he wanted life.

4 Slaves knew that if they ran away, they would be hunted down. They knew the odds of making it to freedom were against them. In a place where all black people were slaves, all white people noticed a black runaway. Unless he had a pass from his master, he had to be a fugitive. Therefore, it was imperative that slaves on the run not be seen. Darkness was the only friend they had.

Daniel and Julian headed for the river through the woods that ran alongside it. The moon was tangled in the dark clouds, and there was nothing left of it but an eerie glow.

Julian led the way with old Jeb's dying words leading him like a beacon: *Follow the river. Don't ever lose sight of the river.*

When Julian was about nine, Ed Whitney had taught him how to find directions. He pointed out the family of stars shaped like a dipper.

"See, yonder," Ed Whitney said, pointing up at the dark sky, "those two stars in the bowl of the dipper. Those are pointers telling you where the North Star is. See it up there, straight off the handle of the dipper? If you face the North Star, you're headed north, and south is behind you."

Julian had been excited by this new information. Almost every night afterward, he'd look for the Big Dipper constellation and then the North Star.

Now the boys hurried into a stand of live oak trees draped with Spanish moss. The boys carried cornmeal cakes, bacon, and their water gourds. Julian had managed to snatch a pocketknife as well from the gin house. He thought it would come in handy for cutting up game or gutting the fish they caught.

Neither Julian nor Daniel had ever lived in the wild before, but they had spent days hunting and fishing with Ed Whitney. Both knew how to build a fire and stalk small game.

"How long you figure it'll take to walk to New Orleans?" Daniel asked.

Like Julian, Daniel had never been to New Orleans. Thomas had told them a lot about it though. All of his stories were exciting. He told about a great port filled with ships coming and going. Some brought sugar from the West Indies and wine from France. Others carried coffee and rosewood and mahogany from Central America. All those places were strange to Julian, almost unbelievable, like distant lands in fairy tales.

But most exciting of all were the stories Thomas told about free people with black skin. They simply walked the streets of New Orleans like white people. There were black slaves in New Orleans, of course. But they looked no different from the free blacks who came and went as they wanted. So a fugitive slave could easily get lost in the crowd.

"It'll take us maybe 15 nights to get to New Orleans," Julian told Daniel. "If we're lucky, and nothing bad happens, that is."

Then Julian told Daniel what Uncle Jeb had told him about the crazy white man who would help them.

"But what if he's not there?" Daniel worried. "Or what if there's no house with a rooster on the roof? Then what?"

"Then we'll find our way by ourselves," Julian said with a bravado he didn't really feel.

"Old Jeb could have remembered it wrong," Daniel pointed out.

"He could have remembered it right too, Daniel," Julian said.

"I can't believe there's a white man who wants to help slaves escape anyway," Daniel muttered. "I guess I'll have to see that to believe it."

He was quiet then, and Julian was glad. He was no more sure of the validity of Jeb's directions than Daniel was. But dwelling on it didn't help matters. They just had to *do* it.

The boys moved on, making good time. But about an hour later, the sounds of yelping dogs filled the night.

"Oh no," Daniel cried, growing weak with terror, "they missed us back at the plantation. And now the slave catchers are coming with bloodhounds. They'll run us down and take us back to the plantation. They'll flay us alive!"

Julian felt the cold hand of terror grip him too, but he tried not to show it. "It's not likely they'll miss us until dawn," he said. "Could be the dogs are out for some other reason. Might be men hunting possum."

"No, it's the patterollers," Daniel groaned.

"Keep moving," Julian said. "We have to reach the river. If the dogs get too close, we'll jump in. Going in the water cuts off the scent."

The boys scrambled through the brush, reaching the bank of the river that meandered south. The yelping of the dogs grew closer.

"What if it's Cannon himself leading the pack?" Daniel said in a trembling voice. "Oh Julian, he almost killed me just for breaking that cotton branch. What's he going to do to us when he finds us?"

"*Come on!*" Julian insisted. "We're almost to the riverbank now."

The boys scrambled down a ravine and huddled near the water, their ears cocked to the cries of the dogs. Julian could imagine the terrible beasts, maddened eyes in their huge heads and jaws dripping saliva. They wouldn't quit until they had found where the scent led.

What if they just set the dogs on them? Julian wondered. What did it feel like to be bitten by a dog?

There was a deep silence as the boys waited. A mosquito buzzed near Julian's ear. Then it landed on his neck and bit hard. But he didn't move to slap it. He didn't want to make a sound.

Finally Daniel whispered, "The sound's moving off, don't you think?"

"I think so," Julian said. "Maybe it was just some farm dogs chasing a raccoon or something."

"You think so, Julian?" Daniel asked.

"I do," Julian said. "Listen, Daniel, we have to be brave. We can't be jumping over every little thing we hear. Or else we'll die of fear before we get to New Orleans. I remember my mama telling me that you can make it through anything if you just put your mind to it. And that's what I plan to do. We've come too far to get caught by our own fears."

"I'm scared of dogs, and I'm scared of patterollers, Julian," Daniel admitted.

"Patterollers are stupid white men, mostly poor," Julian said. "Old Jeb used to laugh about them. They can't get regular jobs that call for a little sense, so they chase down fugitive slaves. But you can trick them if you're smart. Old Jeb said they like to drink corn liquor, and half the time they can't tell a runaway slave from a gum tree."

He listened again. All was quiet. "Come on. Let's go," he said.

They moved on then, following the river south.

"I don't remember my mama," Daniel said suddenly.

"I remember mine," Julian said. "She was real pretty and smelled like violets. She sang sweet too. She would hold me on her lap and sing to me, and she was so soft and nice. Everybody liked her. Even Ed Whitney."

"Master Ed was a good man," Daniel said.

"He was," Julian replied, memories of the Whitney farm flowing across his mind as sweetly as wind over clover. "I remember sometimes for no reason he would bring us all peach tarts. And he would roast a pig or a turkey, and we'd have ourselves a feast."

Daniel nodded. "Yeah, I remember that too. You know, he liked you best of all the boys. Anybody could see that."

Julian nodded, comforted by the sounds of frogs in the night. He had heard once that frogs stopped chirping when something was wrong. But then how would the frogs know the difference between Julian and Daniel tromping through and patterollers? he wondered.

"I sure do wish that old Missus let me say good-bye to Master Ed,"

Julian said. "I'd have liked to tell him how I felt."

"That old woman's going to burn to a crisp in hell," Daniel said. "She sold us north to Mr. Cannon out of pure meanness."

"That's the truth," Julian agreed.

The terrain of the land was uneven now. There were hills to climb and little valleys to slosh through that slowed them down. Julian worried that dawn would come before they found the house with the rooster weather vane. Then they'd have to hide out for the day before moving on. He knew the longer they stayed on the run, the better chance they had of getting caught. If that crazy man could really help them, they needed to reach him soon.

5 The bank of clouds above finally sailed on, exposing the valley to the light of the moon.

"This moonlight is good for getting around," Daniel said. "But they could find us easy in it too."

"Maybe so if they were birds flying over our heads," Julian said, "but they aren't. If we hear anybody coming, we can hide mighty fast in the brush."

"What's that funny word Uncle Jeb told you—about the white folks who don't like slavery?" Daniel asked.

"Abolitionists," Julian said. Julian wished he could read. Then he would know something about such things. But it was against the law to teach a slave to read or write.

Thomas had told him that black people in New Orleans often read and wrote in beautiful script. He said that some of these men wore long black frocks like preachers and spoke with golden tongues. Julian hoped that one day he would learn to read and write too.

"I've never heard that word before,"

Daniel said.

"Me neither," Julian said. "I just hope Uncle Jeb knew what he was talking about."

"I'm getting tired," Daniel said, "and my feet hurt."

"I'm tired too," Julian answered. "But we have to keep moving while it's still dark."

Half an hour later, the sky began to lighten as dawn approached. Julian looked around. There was no sign of the big house with the rooster on the roof. He knew now they had no choice. They would have to hide out for the day.

"Sun's coming up," Julian told Daniel. "We have to find a good hiding place to spend the day. Let's head for that ravine over there. We've got bacon and corn cakes to eat. And we've got water. We can hunker down in the brush and get some sleep. Then, when it gets dark, we'll find the house with the weather vane."

Daniel scrambled through the brush after Julian. They crawled underneath the branches of a willow tree and sat down. It was still fairly dark, but in another 20 minutes the sun would be up.

The boys ate some bacon and corn cakes and then scrunched down to sleep. They took short, nervous naps while the world came to life around them. Every time a wagon rattled in the distance, they awoke and half sat up, ready to run at an instant's notice. Then, about midday, they heard the voices of children in the distance.

Julian peered from their brushy hiding place to see three black children walking barefoot down a path about a hundred yards away. They looked as if they were on some errand.

Daniel joined him and looked out too. "You think it would be safe to ask them about the house with the rooster on the roof?" he asked.

"I don't know," Julian said. "We might frighten them. If we do that, we're sure to get caught." But he knew their chances depended on finding someone to help them. And the only person he knew of was the crazy man in the house with the weather vane. He decided to take a chance. He crept out of the brush and looked back at Daniel. "If things don't go right I'll holler, and then we'll both take off for the river," he whispered.

Julian walked across the field toward the children. Two were little girls who looked to be about five or six years old. They wore faded cotton dresses and tattered ribbons in their hair. One was a boy about nine or ten. As Julian approached, the three looked at him with wary eyes.

"Who are you?" the boy demanded.

Julian smiled and said, "My name is Julian. What's yours?"

"My name is Robert," the boy answered. "These are my sisters."

"Nice to meet you," Julian said to the trio. "My master sent me to find a house with a rooster on the roof. Do you know of such a place?"

Robert nodded. "That'd be the Eckert place. But you don't want to go there. Mister Eckert's crazy."

Julian's heart raced. So there *was* such a place! And such a man! "Is the Eckert place near here?" he asked.

"We'll show you," Robert said, "but we won't go past the gate with you."

Julian hailed Daniel, and the two boys followed the children down a narrow trail that was little more than wagon tracks. Julian glanced around nervously the whole way, expecting some white man to appear behind them.

"How do you know Mr. Eckert is crazy?" Julian asked the boy.

"My mama's got double-sight," the little boy explained. "So she knows. She can see a worrisome spirit. She says Mister Eckert might be Plat-eye himself. You know who Plat-eye is, don't you?"

"I heard tales of Plat-eye when I was your age," Julian smiled. Plat-eye was an evil spirit with fiery eyes who set on travelers in the woods. He was as large as an ox, and nothing could stop him but sulfur or gunpowder. It was a tale the slaves told on cold winter nights around the fire. Julian wasn't worried about Plat-eye though. He was worried about ordinary white men who wanted to put him in chains and send him back to the misery of the cotton plantation.

They came to a clearing then, and Robert pointed and said, "There it is. That's the Eckert place."

In the distance. Julian could see a large, decaying house, half-hidden by trees draped with moss. The gate hung from a single rusty hinge. A weather vane rooster was perched on the roof.

"We're not going any farther," Robert said.

"Thank you, Robert," Julian said. "You've helped us a lot."

The boy looked Julian and Daniel up and down for a minute, and then he said, "You're running, aren't you?"

Julian hesitated. It was obvious Robert knew what they were up to. If he lied to him, it would make them even more suspicious in the boy's eyes. He decided to tell the truth.

"Yeah, we're running, Robert," he

said, kneeling before the child. "But you can't tell anyone. Not even your mama. Do you understand?"

Robert suddenly looked sad. "I won't say anything," he said. "My daddy ran last year. The dogs ran him into the river. He drowned."

Julian heard Daniel let out a long, sad sigh behind him. "We're real sorry about your daddy, Robert," Julian said. "But you take good care of your mama, you hear? You're the man in the family now, aren't you?"

Robert brightened a little and said, "I will. I'll take good care of her. And we won't tell anyone about seeing you." He took his sisters' hands then, and the three of them ran down the wagon wheel trail and out of sight.

"Let's go," Julian said. He headed toward the house with Daniel following.

"I still don't feel right about this," Daniel said as they walked. "How are we going to know what we're getting into? Maybe that Eckert man is waiting behind the door with a hatchet. They said he was crazy, you know."

"We've come this far, Daniel," Julian said. "We've got to see it through. Let's just be careful."

The boys went through a creaking gate and then crept toward the big front porch. The closer they got to the house, the more dilapidated it looked. The shutters hung like crooked teeth, and boards were missing from the steps and the porch.

"Maybe nobody even lives here, Julian," Daniel said. "It sure doesn't look lived in."

Just then the sound of a wagon coming down the road reached their ears. The wagon was coming fast. The hooves of the horses were striking the hard-packed road like rifle balls.

"Maybe those children told," Daniel gasped.

"No, I don't think they'd do that," Julian said. "Get down!"

Julian and Daniel huddled in the brush near the front of the house. A few scrawny chickens pecked at the

earth around them. At that moment
two large dogs came bounding from
the woods to greet the wagon. They
had massive, lion-sized heads. Julian
thought how lucky they were that
these beasts had not spotted them as
they had approached the house.

"We're cornered!" Daniel whispered.

"Don't move!" Julian hissed.

The wagon slowed as it came
around the corner.

Julian shuddered, wondering if the
children *had* said something to betray
them. Maybe Robert's sisters
mentioned seeing two black men in
the woods. And now maybe this
wagon brought slave catchers
who were determined to take the
boys back.

Julian could already see Cyrus
Cannon's evil face sneering with glee
as they were dragged back to the
plantation in chains. Julian could feel
the whip, the pain, the blood running
down his back. "Thought you could
get away, eh?" Cannon would say,
taking pleasure in every lash he

delivered. "Thought you could outsmart me, eh?"

"Pompey! Caesar!" the man who drove the wagon shouted. The dogs romped out to meet their master, and Julian and Daniel finally caught sight of him. He was a tall, skinny man with a straggly gray beard that reached to his belt buckle. His hair was also gray, and it flowed down his back like wisps of smoke. He wore a dirty black coat and worn black trousers.

"What now?" Daniel whispered.

Julian wasn't sure what to do. The man was white. That said a lot right there. But this man sure looked like the man Uncle Jeb had described. His instinct told him that the old man could be trusted. He decided it was time to find out. He stood up and, in a thin, shaky voice, said, "Mister Eckert?"

Immediately the two dogs, hackles raised, raced toward Julian. He glanced down at Daniel's terror-stricken face. "Don't move!" Julian said.

"Pompey! Caesar!" the old man called. The dogs froze in their tracks. "I'm Levi Eckert," he said. "Who are you?"

Julian signaled for Daniel to stand up. "We're fugitives, sir," Julian said as politely as he could. "We're trying to get to New Orleans. Someone told me you might be able to help us."

The old man's eyes gleamed like two hot coals. His bushy brows stuck out like porcupine quills. He certainly looks crazy, Julian thought.

"Inside the house with you!" he commanded. He led the way onto the porch, and Julian and Daniel followed. The old floorboards wheezed and creaked beneath them.

When they were all inside, the man said, "How did you hear of me?"

"Jebediah Samson. He said to look for the house with the rooster on the roof," Julian said. "He said you were an abolitionist."

"Is old Jeb still alive?" Eckert asked.

"No," Julian said. "He died a while back."

Eckert nodded. "Then he never tasted freedom. Too bad."

Julian and Daniel sat down at a large table covered with a tattered linen cloth. The cloth was faded, and the edges were frayed. But a chipped vase with fresh flowers sat in the center of the table.

Just then a woman entered the room. She was about 60 with a plump face and gray hair tied up in a bun.

"Esther," Mr. Eckert said, "can you bring us something to eat? We got two hungry boys here. They're on the run."

Esther greeted Julian and Daniel warmly and promised to return with food.

"Begging your pardon, sir," Julian said. "But shouldn't we maybe hide or something? What if someone comes?"

"Here?" Mr. Eckert laughed. "Why, no one comes here. They all think I'm crazy. Now, tell me about yourselves."

Julian understood now. Mr. Eckert acted as if he were crazy to cover up his activities. Julian was starting to trust this man.

Together Julian and Daniel told Mr. Eckert about the Whitney farm and how they were sold north after Ed Whitney died. They showed him their whip-scarred backs. The wounds were healing, but there would be scars for as long as they lived.

A little while later, Esther brought dishes laden with meat and vegetables. Julian hadn't seen such good food since he'd left the Whitney farm. As they ate, Mr. Eckert said, "You say you're heading south, to New Orleans?"

"Yes," Julian answered, cutting a piece of meat. "A friend of ours said that slaves can hide among free blacks there."

"Bad idea," Levi Eckert said, shaking his head. "You need to head north where there's no slavery."

"North? How far?" Julian asked.

"About a thousand miles," Eckert said matter-of-factly.

"A thousand miles?" Daniel echoed. "We could never walk that far."

"You don't walk the whole way,

Daniel," the older man said. "You go by the Underground Railroad."

Both boys chuckled. "Never heard of a train that takes slaves to freedom," Julian said.

"It's not a train," Eckert said. "It's a system of hiding places between here and Illinois. Folks like me and Esther help you along the way. Sometimes you ride in a hay wagon, and sometimes you ride in a funeral procession. Sometimes you walk. The Underground Railroad's been in operation for more than 20 years. It follows the Mississippi up to Illinois. Once you cross the Ohio River into Illinois, you're free."

"You mean really *free?*" Julian asked. "Nobody can snatch us and send us back to Cannon's plantation?"

Levi Eckert frowned. "It's not quite that easy," he said. "There's a thing called the Fugitive Slave Act. It allows them to grab you anywhere, even in the North, and take you back. But thousands of slaves have eluded capture, and they're living free right now. You just have to be careful. Don't trust men easily once you cross the Ohio River."

Julian couldn't believe his ears. A whole system set up to help him and Daniel to freedom! He put down his fork and breathed a sigh of relief. Maybe they would make it after all.

That day Julian and Daniel slept in real beds with soft mattresses and comforters. The beds seemed like clouds of silk compared to the planks at the Cannon plantation. They slept hard the rest of the day and into the evening. Both boys were worn out from running nearly all night long.

When darkness began to fall, Eckert roused the boys for the beginning of their trip north on the Underground Railroad. Eckert gave them both shirts and trousers. Esther brought them sacks of food for the journey. They were about to leave when they heard the shatter of glass. A large rock had crashed through the front window of the house.

Wild laughter followed the rock's

path. Immediately Julian envisioned a mob outside the house. The slave catchers were no doubt among them.

Levi Eckert plucked the linen cloth off the table and wrapped it around him. Then he snatched a burning hickory stick from the stove and flung open the front door. "Death and damnation!" he screamed into the dusky evening, wielding the burning stick like a torch.

6

Three white boys fled from the property, stumbling over one another as they scrambled off.

"That ought to keep them away for a while," Eckert laughed. "They'll swear they've seen a demon. But they'll tell their friends how brave they were, how they stood up to it." He let out a delighted cackle.

"I don't know, Julian," Daniel whispered. "Sometimes that old man sure looks crazy."

"It doesn't matter if he is or isn't," Julian answered. "As long as he'll help us."

That night, Julian and Daniel hid in a wagon that rattled north driven by Mr. Eckert. It was loaded down with vegetables and old clothing. Before dawn Eckert came to a small farmhouse, and the boys spent the day there with instructions for the next part of the journey.

Two nights later they crossed into Arkansas in a dead wagon that moved north to a cemetery. They were accompanied by two men who sang doleful songs all the way.

Just before dawn, the wagon reached the cemetery. The boys hid all day. When darkness fell, a man arrived and led them on foot through the swampland along the Mississippi. That night they were taken across the Arkansas river. The boatman didn't say much, but the boys knew he was on their side. Once on land, they moved in the darkness until they reached an empty cabin where they took refuge.

As the boys ate in the cabin, Daniel asked, "Julian, you think someday you might find a woman and marry her?"

Julian shrugged his shoulders. "Maybe."

"You remember Lettie, that girl who lived on the Hawkinses' farm?" Daniel asked. "She was pretty, wasn't she? She had the nicest face."

Julian nodded. "You liked her, didn't you, Daniel?" he said, smiling to encourage Daniel to continue.

"I sure did," Daniel replied. "But she was a good house slave. The Hawkinses never would sell her to Mr. Whitney."

"When we get across the Ohio River, Daniel, we're going to be free," Julian said. "We can find pretty women for ourselves. We won't need anybody buying them for us. We can do what white folks do—court somebody and then marry her."

"I saw two slaves get married once," Daniel said. "The two of them just jumped over a broomstick and that made them Mister and Missus. Didn't look right to me. White folks don't marry that way."

"It's not going to be that way with us, Daniel," Julian said. "We'll get married the right way, in a church." He sighed and stretched his aching legs. He was bone-tired and sore from the journey. But he was also happier than he had ever been. At the safe houses the food was good, and they were allowed plenty of rest. But that wasn't the main thing. The main thing was that freedom was getting closer every day. It was out there waiting for them. He could taste it when he ate a hot biscuit given to him by the hands of a white woman. He could smell it in the wind from distant pine woods. He could hear it in the wild shrieks of white owls as they swooped from tree to tree. Julian was fairly bursting with the whole idea of freedom. It was like a miracle unfolding before his eyes.

The next night, the pair moved alone through the woods by a river, following the directions they had been given at the last safe house. For more than a week now they had moved swiftly and without problems. But they were still in Arkansas, slave territory, and Missouri lay ahead. Missouri was a slave state too, but they only had to cross a little piece of that state.

Suddenly they were startled by voices behind them. Daniel glanced fearfully at Julian. "Cannon!" he whispered.

"Come on! Let's hide over there where the trees are thick," Julian whispered back.

Then they heard dogs baying in the darkness.

"Bloodhounds!" Daniel said.

"They've got bloodhounds, Julian!"

"To the river! Hurry!" Julian cried.

The boys ran for the river so they could lose their scent before the bloodhounds reached them. But the voices were approaching rapidly.

Julian glanced over his shoulder. About a hundred yards away, two men and a boy approached. One of the men held a lantern, and the other held two dogs on leashes. The dogs strained mightily against the ropes, eager to pursue their prey.

"Run!" Julian screamed at Daniel, but Daniel stumbled when his foot sank into the soft earth near the river. He went down. Julian dragged Daniel to his feet, and they continued their mad dash to the river. But the few seconds it took for Daniel to recover his footing were costly. It brought them within shooting range of the rifle held by one of the men.

"You want to stop, or you want to be dead?" the man yelled.

Julian stared longingly at the river. Even in the darkness, he could tell they were only a few yards away. Maybe, he thought desperately, they ought to just make a break for it and risk death.

As if he had read Julian's mind, the man with the rifle shouted, "You move a muscle, darky, and I swear I'll blow your head off."

Julian and Daniel froze. As the three approached, the man with the rifle said to the boy, "Get out the rope, you lazy, good-for-nothing leech. We don't want to lose these two young bucks. They're going to bring us a good bounty."

Julian scrutinized his captors. The man holding the rifle was bushy-haired with a short brown beard. He wore a ragged red flannel shirt and trousers held up with a piece of rope. His sneering smile revealed dingy gray teeth. And the hands that held the rifle looked as if they hadn't been washed in days.

The man holding the dogs was small and almost bald. He had a handlebar mustache and a stubble of a beard. His clothes were as dirty, if not dirtier, than the other man's. Julian could smell the whiskey on his breath from where he stood six feet away.

Slave catchers for sure, Julian thought.

The boy was about 14. He had a sallow complexion and was obviously underfed. He wore an old straw hat that was too large and kept slipping down over his eyes. His clothes were rags, and he was barefoot. Julian watched the boy carry over the two ropes. He could see that the youth was nervous, almost frightened.

The bald man handed the two leashes to the boy. Then he took the ropes and tied Julian and Daniel to two trees. He made the ropes so tight that the pain shot up to Julian's shoulders.

"How much bounty you figure we'll get for the two of 'em?" the bald man asked the man with the rifle.

The man scratched his face and said, "Enough to lay low for a while and drink plenty of whiskey, I reckon."

"Yippee!" the bald man cried. "I'll take the dogs back to town now. You bring those two in to Mr. Webb in the morning. He's got all the posters from the slave owners. He'll know what to pay us right off." He took the dogs from the boy and headed down the road. Julian could hear the dogs baying as the bald man disappeared into the night.

"Where'd you darkies run from?" the man with the rifle asked.

"We're not running," Julian lied. "We've got passes from our master to buy supplies in Missouri."

"And just whereabouts are those passes?" the man asked.

Julian thought fast. "We lost them when we fell in the river," he said.

"I'll just bet you did," the man laughed.

"Are we spending the night here, Zeke?" the scrawny boy asked.

"Yeah, Joshua, we are, as if it's any concern of yours," the man answered. "Then bright and early when Mr. Webb's open for business, we'll take

these two into town. Now get a fire
going."

Julian closed his eyes and fought
down the frustration that was rising
within him. He felt as if he'd been
caught in a nightmare. Just when
freedom seemed so close, it had been
snatched away, maybe forever.

Zeke started a pot of coffee brewing
over the fire. Then he brought out
some hardtack bread and jerky.

"I'm hungry," Joshua said softly.

"Too bad," Zeke said. "Ain't enough
for me and you both. Now fetch me a
cup from that bag."

The boy dug into the same bag he
had gotten the ropes from. He
produced an old blue tin cup with no
handle.

"Pour me some coffee," Zeke
ordered. Joshua took a rag from the
bag and picked up the coffee pot. As
he started to pour, the pot became too
hot even through the rag. He dropped
the pot, spilling the coffee out onto the
ground.

"Now look what you done!" Zeke

yelled. He raised his hand as if to strike the boy, but Joshua moved out of the way just in time. Evidently Zeke was too lazy to pursue him. Instead he yelled again. "I wish to heaven I'd never married your ma and got stuck with a worthless fool like you! Now get to bed! And stay as far away from me as possible!"

Silently the boy picked up a bedroll and carried it toward a pile of rocks. In the light cast by the fire, Julian noticed something stirring by the rock pile. It looked like a prairie rattler.

"Rattler over there!" Julian yelled.

Joshua jumped back in terror, seconds before he would have riled the rattler by throwing a blanket on top of him. The snake slithered off into the night. Obviously shaken, the boy looked at Julian, but he said nothing.

"Curse you," the man spat at Julian. "You should have let him do it. Then I'd be rid of him for good."

Julian felt the bark of the tree behind him with his fingers. It was very rough. If he rubbed his ropes against it, maybe the ropes would fray and he could pull loose. Julian still had the pocketknife in his trousers he had stolen from the Cannon plantation, but he couldn't get to it. But once he was free, he could use it to cut Daniel loose and, if need be, defend himself against the slave catcher.

He glanced at his friend. Daniel looked broken in spirit. He slumped in his bonds hopelessly. He knew what Daniel was feeling, and he ached for his friend. I'll get us free, Julian vowed. I will!

Once Zeke fell asleep, Joshua moved his blanket roll near the fire and lay down. Soon Zeke was snoring loudly, and the boy's chest was rising up and down as if he were asleep. Julian began to work on the ropes binding his hands. He moved his hands up and down, forcing the rope fiber against the bark. As he did, his wrists became so sore that each motion was an agony. He felt the blood trickling from his broken flesh, but he kept at it. Each time the pain became unbearable, he stopped for a minute, then continued the effort.

Freedom, Julian kept thinking. Freedom. The chance to be his own man. Why not? Why should white men be free while black men were kept in bondage, robbed of their dignity and their pride? He wouldn't go back to being a slave. He was not an animal, and he wouldn't allow himself to be treated like one. He'd rather die first.

Julian glanced at the horizon. With terror, he saw that the sky was beginning to lighten. When dawn came, all hope would be lost. Zeke would awaken then, and the two boys would be doomed. Up and down, up and down he moved the rope. But the fibers refused to give. Again and again Julian tested the rope, but it was like steel. Maybe, Julian thought in despair, it was impossible to break it.

Julian stole quick, desperate glances at the sky. He worked harder, jamming the rope against the rough bark with frantic effort. The pain didn't matter anymore. No amount of pain

mattered. Still the rope would not
yield.

Julian looked up then to see Joshua
awake and staring at him. The boy got
up slowly and came over. He looked at
Julian's frayed bindings. Then he
looked over at Zeke, who was still
snoring loudly. Julian was afraid he
would wake the man.

"Help me, Joshua," Julian whispered.
"Help me like I helped you."

Joshua looked back at Julian. He
hesitated and glanced over at the
sleeping man again. Suddenly, without
a word, the boy took out a knife and
crouched behind Julian, slashing
through the fibers still binding him to
the tree.

Julian leaped up. His heart thumped
and pounded like a large wild bird
under his shirt. He rushed to Daniel,
who slept slumped over halfway to the
ground. Julian covered Daniel's mouth
with his hand so he wouldn't cry out in
surprise. Then he took out his knife
and cut his friend free.

Daniel staggered to his feet,

disoriented. Julian could see that he wasn't sure if this were reality or a dream. Julian quickly raised his finger to his lips. "Shhh!" he warned.

Julian stood there a moment, clutching his pocketknife, his wrists throbbing with pain, his eyes on the sleeping slave catcher. The sensible thing to do was to put an end to the man with a quick thrust of his knife. But even as he thought it, he knew he couldn't do it.

He turned to Joshua. "Thank you," he whispered.

The boy nodded.

"Now get back in your sleeping roll," Julian said. "Pretend you've been asleep." The boy returned to his place by the fire.

Daniel was looking at Julian, waiting for direction. Julian raised his arm and pointed north. As the boys sprinted from the clearing, Julian turned once and looked back at the young white boy. Joshua waved as Julian and Daniel raced for the trees that lined the river.

7 As they ran, Julian glanced at Daniel. He was lagging behind. "Faster!" Julian urged.

"My legs!" Daniel cried. He stopped and rubbed one of his calves.

"You've just got cramps from sleeping against that tree all night," Julian said. "Keep moving, Daniel. The cramps will work themselves out. Come on!"

Limping, Daniel started to run again. Half an hour later, Julian finally signaled for them to stop. Daniel sank to his knees and lay panting on the ground. Julian figured they'd put at least two miles between themselves and the slave catcher. And without the dogs, it would be hard to track them.

As he leaned breathlessly against a tree, Julian thought about the white boy who had helped them. He hoped the boy was safe and that Zeke would never find out about his part in their escape. He wondered if he should have killed the slave catcher. He surely hated him enough to kill him. But he remembered something his mother had taught him many years ago. His mother had told him never to take a life unless there was no other way to stay alive. He didn't remember thinking it as he stood over the sleeping slave catcher. But deep down, he must have.

They walked another two miles and then found a place to sleep. To continue traveling by daylight was too dangerous.

That night around midnight, they reached the next safe house. This time it was a shack lying half-buried in a willow-bordered stream. The silver foliage of the buffalo bush and gray-green sage covered the brown, sandy earth around the shack. A young white man with curly dark hair welcomed them in with mugs of cool apple cider. He introduced himself as Jim Potter. He asked Julian and Daniel about themselves, and they told him they had escaped from the Cannon plantation.

"I know of the place," Potter said. "Cannon is an evil man." Then he started denouncing slavery with such fury, it seemed that he himself had suffered it. "There must be a rebellion that destroys the institution of slavery," he stormed. "I would take up arms myself."

Julian and Daniel looked at each other, not sure what to think of the young man.

The curly-haired man continued, "Nat Turner had the right idea."

"Who was Nat Turner?" Daniel asked.

"A slave who led a rebellion," Potter explained. "He killed every white person in the household. And many others besides. Can you blame him? There's no such thing as a good slave owner."

"I knew a good one once," Julian said, remembering Ed Whitney.

The young man took another swig of cider and looked hard at Julian. "How is it then that you were sold to one of the most brutal slave masters by this kind-hearted man?" he asked.

"Mr. Whitney died, and his wife sold us," Julian said. "She hated us slaves, but she hated me the most. And Mr. Whitney—he seemed to like me more than the others."

Daniel nodded.

The man leaned over the cider barrel then and asked, "Who was your father, Julian?"

Julian shrugged. He had never thought much about his father. Many slave children did not know who their fathers were. Husbands and wives were often sold off in different directions. The fact that they were married to each other made little difference to the owner. When Julian was small his mother had told him just that—that his father had been sold to another plantation shortly after he was born.

"I don't know who my father was," he answered. "I'm known by the name of Holland, so maybe that was his name, but I never met him."

"I'm called Jim Potter," the young man said, "but my father has a different name. My father is a prosperous banker in Boston. And my mother was a free black woman. Look at my hair, Julian. Look at my skin. My mother was black, and my father was white. Just like you."

The words rocked Julian back on his heels. "Like me? What are you saying? My father was a slave . . ." Julian's voice trailed off.

Potter jumped up and took a lone book off a shelf. "Look at this book," he told Julian.

"I can't read," Julian said.

"Just look at the picture at the front," Jim said. He handed the open book to Julian.

Julian looked down and saw the portrait of a handsome young black man. His hair was short and curly. He had a broad nose and piercing eyes, and he wore a fine suit. He looked like an important man. "Who is this?" Julian asked.

"Frederick Douglass," Potter explained. "Surely you've heard of this great antislavery orator?"

Julian shook his head, "No, I've never heard of him."

"He wrote this book," Potter said. "It's called *My Bondage and My Freedom*. It's about his escape from slavery and his efforts to end slavery. He, too, is part black and part white. When I look at his face, I see the same mixture of races as I see in your face and in mine."

Julian shook his head. "No, my father was . . ." But then he thought back to the Whitney farm. Memories flooded over him like a river. Ed Whitney always there, favoring him. Ed Whitney sitting under an oak tree with Julian's mother, laughing and talking. Ed Whitney at his mother's grave, his face filled with sorrow. Julian had made little of it at the time because he had been so young. Now he said, "I guess maybe that's why he was partial to me. And I guess that's why the Missus hated me so. I was his son, and she wanted Howard to be Mr. Whitney's only son."

Tears filled Julian's eyes. Before he had been saddened by the death of a man who was like a grandfather to him. Now he mourned the death of his father. Daniel reached over and laid his hand on Julian's shoulder.

The next day, curled up in sleep on the floor of the shack, Julian drifted in and out of troublesome dreams. He thought about the man who was his father. Why had his mother never told him? Why had Ed Whitney never let on?

More than likely, he was ashamed of me, Julian thought sadly. Or maybe it was out of deference for Mrs. Whitney. After all, she was his wife.

* * *

A wagon with Julian and Daniel hiding in the back rolled toward the border of Illinois that dark, moonless night. Right over the water was freedom. All they had to do was cross the Mississippi and then take the Ohio River to Cairo, Illinois.

Julian and Daniel climbed from the wagon and boarded a small boat with two other fugitive slaves. They, too, had come north by way of the Underground Railroad.

As the boat glided noiselessly through the water, they could see lights flickering in windows on the other side. Julian knew those were candles burning in people's homes. He wondered if they knew how lucky they were to live in Illinois—a free state.

Julian's heart drummed in his chest as they approached the Illinois shore. He could hear Daniel breathing heavily in the darkness beside him. He glanced at the other two fugitives. Their heads were bowed, and their hands were folded in prayer.

The boatman skillfully guided the small craft into an area of tall weeds by the shore. He jumped from the boat and tied it to the slim trunk of a sandbar willow tree. "Come on, folks," he said. "This is it."

For a moment no one moved. Julian felt as if he were in a dream. As long as he stayed still, the dream would continue. If he moved, it might end—and he might wake up back at the Cannon plantation.

Finally Daniel nudged Julian in the side. "Let's go," he said.

Slowly Julian stepped from the boat onto solid ground. He stared up at the sky. It looked the same, but it wasn't the same. It was the first time he had seen the sky as a free man. The earth beneath his feet was the same earth, but it, too, was different. He had never stood on it as a free man.

Julian grabbed hold of Daniel's arm. "We're free!" he said.

"Hallelujah!" Daniel said.

"We can do what we want, Daniel," Julian said. "We're the same as anybody else."

The boatman laid a hand on Julian's arm. "Take it easy, young man. You're free now. You're in Illinois, and there's no slavery here. But you're still black. It's not going to be as easy as you might think."

Julian took a deep breath. He was inhaling freedom. He savored the smell of it. He opened his mouth and

let the dewy dawn drop on his tongue.
He was tasting freedom, and it was
sweet and delicious.

Julian looked at the boatman. "But
I'm free," he said, "and freedom knows
no color."

8 The boatman led Julian, Daniel, and his two other passengers to a rooming house. The house was in a section of Cairo where most of the people were black. It was run by a black woman named Caroline Lawton.

Caroline Lawton was a widow in her forties. She welcomed fugitive slaves and let them live at the boardinghouse at no charge until they got jobs and could pay.

"So what do you boys plan on doing now that you're free?" Mrs. Lawton asked Julian and Daniel at dinner later that day.

"I haven't really thought about it," Julian admitted. "I didn't dare plan anything in case things didn't work out for us."

"Lots of boys like you go to work for white people," Mrs. Lawton offered. "They need servants to drive their carriages or take care of their houses. It's good, honest work, and the pay is fair."

Julian shook his head obstinately. "I'm through being a servant for white folks," he said. "I want to learn a skill like carpentry or blacksmithing. Then I'm going to get me a *real* job."

"Many people in this town won't hire black men," Mrs. Lawton warned. "Being free doesn't make you equal in their minds."

Julian thought about what the boatman had said, *You're still black.*

Just then Mrs. Lawton's daughter, Dinah, came into the room. She was a slim girl about the same age as Julian. She wasn't overly pretty, but Julian noticed right away that she had kind eyes.

Mrs. Lawton introduced her and then said, "Tell the boys about your job, Dinah."

Dinah smiled. "I'm a maid at the Marston house," she said. "I'm an upstairs girl. I make good wages, and sometimes Mrs. Marston gives me gifts like clothes she doesn't want anymore. She's very kind, and so is her husband. Mr. Marston's one of the finest men in town."

"But that's almost like slave work," Julian said. "Don't you want a real job?"

Dinah shrugged and said, "I might

like to have a different kind of job. I'd get better wages if I was a cashier in a store. But they don't want girls with dark skin. Besides, Mr. and Mrs. Marston have been good to me. They like me, and I like them."

Daniel had been quiet through the conversation. Now he asked, "Do you think the Marstons might hire me?"

"They might be able to use you in their stable," Dinah answered. "Hank is in charge of the stable and the horses, but his health is failing. He's not as reliable as he used to be."

"I know about horses and mules," Daniel said eagerly. "I took care of them at the Whitney farm." He turned to Julian. "Maybe we could both find work at the Marstons', Julian."

"I told you," Julian snapped, "I'm not being a servant."

Daniel shrugged. Then he looked hopefully at Dinah. "Maybe tomorrow you can take me there," he said.

"I'd be glad to, Daniel," Dinah said. "The Marstons are always willing to give somebody a chance. Sure you won't come along, Julian?"

"No, thanks," Julian said. "I'm going

to head out on my own." He couldn't believe any free Negro would want to work as a servant for white people. That was too much like slavery in his mind. And Julian wanted to get as far away from that as possible.

* * *

Julian set out alone the next day. One of Mrs. Lawton's boarders had given him auspicious news. He'd told Julian that a crew of carpenters was building some houses on a street about a mile away. Julian went down there early and looked for the boss.

"Hello!" Julian called to two white carpenters who were sawing on a large timber. "I'm looking for the man who does the hiring."

The men looked coldly at Julian. Neither said a word. But one of them pointed to a man about 50 who stood a few yards away. Then without saying a word, the men returned to their sawing.

As Julian approached the boss, he noticed that the man seemed to have no neck at all. His round little head sat on his shoulders like a pumpkin.

Julian smiled and held out his hand. "I'm looking to be an apprentice carpenter, sir," he said in a polite and friendly manner. "I've got experience. I built chicken houses and fences, and I helped raise a barn at . . . well, where I used to work."

The boss ignored Julian's hand and looked him over. Then he said, "Take a look around you, boy. How many men you see around here who look like you?"

Julian saw about 20 men, mostly young, but some older and more experienced. He could see by the clumsy way the younger ones acted that they were apprentices. These men were toting things for the more experienced men or doing the dirty, hard work that the older ones didn't want to do. But all the men had one thing in common—they were all white.

"I don't see any black men working here, sir," he admitted, "but I could be the first. I can tell you this—you wouldn't be sorry if you hired me. I'd give you the best day's work of any man here."

The boss nodded and said, "That may

be so, boy. But if I hire you, most of my men will walk off the job. And that's the truth. White men aren't willing to work with a black man."

Julian watched the carpenters toiling and sweating in the hot sun. It wasn't easy work, but he wouldn't mind. There was dignity in it. It was skilled work, and it was a man's work. And he envied the men who got the chance to do it. How he wanted to saw up those timbers and hammer those nails into place—to see a house rise up that he'd had a hand in building!

All Julian wanted was a chance to bust his back doing a free man's work. He was about to tell the boss that when the boss said, "Now you'd better get going before the men get riled up and run you off. They got their pride, you know."

"I got mine too," Julian said, walking away.

* * *

"I got the job at the Marston house," Daniel said cheerfully at supper that night. "I'm going to help Mr. Hank take

care of the horses. Mr. Marston told me
Mr. Hank isn't so reliable anymore. But
Mr. Marston doesn't want to turn the
man out because he's been with them
for a long time."

Mrs. Lawton piled pork and yams
onto the plates and smiled at Daniel.
"Good for you, Daniel. Now you just do
your best on that job. But watch out for
Percy Marston. He's Mr. Marston's son.
Percy thinks his father is too soft on
the help and that the old man pays
them too much. Percy's afraid his
father is squandering away his
inheritance. Mind your step when that
man's around."

"I'll be careful," Daniel said, scooping
up a big bite of pork onto his fork. "Mr.
Marston's going to pay me three dollars
a week," he added proudly.

"How about you, Julian?" Dinah
asked. "Did you have any luck
finding work?"

"No," Julian said glumly. "I went to
four places. They were all hiring, but
they didn't want a black man to work
for them."

"Mr. Marston might hire you to drive
his carriage," Daniel said.

"How many times do I have to tell you that I don't want a servant's job?" Julian said sharply.

Mrs. Lawton looked at Julian. "Julian, I think it's fine that you want to learn a trade," she began. "But you have to wake up to the fact that it might not happen right away. Just because this is a free state doesn't mean everybody here's an abolitionist. You're on your own here. You might have to take what you can get until something better comes along."

Julian turned to Daniel. "Sorry," Julian said. "I didn't mean to jump on you. But I aim to get me a real job, and I won't give up till I do. I went to a wagon works today. The old man in charge was closing up shop when I got there. He didn't have time to talk to me. But I'm going back tomorrow, see if he'll have me."

That night, Julian stood outside the boardinghouse, staring up at the sky. He spotted the Big Dipper and then the North Star that had guided him to freedom. He sighed. What kind of freedom would it be? he wondered. Would he end up fetching and toting for the Marstons? He shook his head. No, he couldn't do that. If he did that, he might just as well be back at the Cannon plantation. Julian was his own man now, and he was determined to get a man's job, no matter what it took. Perhaps if he could learn to read and write. Then maybe someone would be more likely to hire him. But where would he learn reading and writing? He was too old to go to school with children. He was still deliberating when a voice came out of the darkness.

"Hello, Julian." Julian turned to see Dinah Lawton coming out of the house. "Getting some fresh air?" she asked.

"Uh-huh," Julian said.

"I came out for some air too," Dinah said. "What are you thinking about?"

Julian hesitated. He was embarrassed to tell her his thoughts. He didn't want her to know that he couldn't read or write.

"Just thinking about getting a job," Julian said.

"So you're going back to the wagon works tomorrow?" the girl asked.

"Yeah," Julian sighed. "But I'll be surprised if he'll even talk to me."

"I was thinking, Julian," Dinah said. "You say the wagon maker is an old man?"

"About 70, I'd guess," Julian replied.

"And he works there alone?" Dinah asked.

"I think so. I didn't see anyone else about," Julian said.

"Then chances are that he needs someone to help him," Dinah said. "What if you offered to work for him for, say, two weeks without pay?"

Julian frowned and asked, "Why would I do that?"

"To show him what a hard worker you are," Dinah answered. "Tell him that if he likes you after two weeks, he can hire you. If not, you'll be on your way. At least you'll get your foot in the door."

What a great idea! Julian thought. Why didn't I think of that? He looked at Dinah. "I'm going to do just that," he said. "Say, you're pretty smart."

The girl smiled, her white teeth flashing in the light from the window. "Thanks. But you probably would have thought of it sooner or later. You seem pretty smart yourself."

Julian shook his head. He felt comfortable with Dinah now and decided to tell her about his lack of schooling. "No, I can't even read or write," he said.

Dinah looked surprised. "Didn't you go to school at the plantation?"

Julian laughed. "It's against the law to teach a slave," he said.

Dinah was quiet for a moment. Then she said softly, "I could teach you, Julian."

"You mean it?" he said. "You'd be willing to do that?"

"Sure," Dinah answered. "In fact, I'd like to. When would you like to start?"

Julian shrugged. "How about now? I've got nothing else to do."

"All right then," Dinah said. "We can work out here. I'll go get a lamp."

A few minutes later, the two were settled on the steps of the porch. "We have to start with the alphabet, Julian," Dinah explained. "You know, *A, B, C.*"

Julian nodded.

Dinah handed Julian a piece of paper and a pencil. Then she opened a book called *Websters Spelling Book* and showed him the letters within. She taught him how to write *A*, *B*, *C*, *D*, and *E*.

Julian labored over the letters until he got them right.

"Now I'm going to show you how to write a word," Dinah said.

"So soon?" Julian asked in wonder. "I've only just started."

Dinah laughed. "What do you sleep on, Julian?" she asked.

"I sleep on a bed now," Julian replied.

"All right, write it," Dinah said. "*B-E-D*. Bed."

Julian wrote the word and stared at it. "You mean that says bed?" he asked.

Dinah laughed and nodded. "See? Already you can write a word, Julian!"

Julian was thrilled. He'd had no idea it was this easy. "Dinah, will you help me every night like this?" he asked.

"Yes, I will," Dinah promised.

Julian couldn't believe his good fortune. Thanks to Dinah, he had a chance of getting a job. And he was learning to read and write!

9 In the morning as the sun was coming up, Julian headed for the wagon maker's shop. He wanted to talk to the old man before he became busy.

"Hello," Julian called out.

The wagon maker was just unlocking the door to the shop. He turned and looked at Julian. "What do you want?" he asked in an unfriendly voice.

"I need work," Julian said. "I'm strong, and I can learn to do anything."

The old man scratched his head of curly gray hair. "I don't need anybody," he said.

Julian came closer and offered his hand. "My name is Julian," he said.

Reluctantly, the wagon maker reached out and shook Julian's hand. "Last's the name," he said.

That's a start, Julian thought.

"Mr. Last, I've worked on wagons," Julian said. "I've run a forge, and I've replaced wheels. I could be a big help to you here."

"I can't afford anybody," Mr. Last said.

Julian glanced around the place. Broken wagons and wheels lay all over the property waiting to be fixed. The elderly man probably didn't make much money working on his own. But if he had a strong, young man to help him, he could double, maybe even triple, his profits.

"I won't cost you anything—for two weeks," Julian offered. "I'll work for no wages at all. Then if I've helped your business, you can hire me. If not, I'll be on my way."

Mr. Last said nothing.

"I'm honest and I'm hardworking, Mr. Last," Julian continued. "And I'll do just about anything."

Ben Last scratched the stubble on his chin. "No wages for two weeks, you say?" he repeated.

"Yes, sir," Julian said, hope rising within him.

The older man glanced around at all the work waiting to be done. "All right then," he said. "You can work for nothing if you're of a mind to. If you're useful, then you've got yourself a job. But if you're as worthless as the others I've had in here over the years, then you're on your way with no fuss, you hear?"

"It's a deal," Julian said.

Mr. Last spat a stream of tobacco juice and said, "What'd you say your name was?"

"Julian Hol—" Julian began, stopping himself. "Julian Whitney." It was the first time he had used his father's name. He would use it from now on. It was his right, his birthright.

Julian hurried into the wagon maker's shop.

For the next two weeks, the old man barked orders at Julian, cursed him, and chastised him for his mistakes. Through it all, Julian struggled to learn the rudiments of wagon making. At the end of each day, his whole body ached from hoisting wagons off the ground and wrestling the wheels loose.

After two weeks, Julian surveyed the yard surrounding the shop. Mr. Last had made considerable progress with Julian's help. He hoped the old man would offer him a job.

"I'll be leaving now, Mr. Last," Julian said at sundown. "Did you want me to come back tomorrow, sir?"

Mr. Last spat a stream of tobacco

juice at the forge, making it sizzle. Then he looked at Julian. "I'll pay you four dollars a week and not a cent more," he said cantankerously. "Take it or leave it."

"I'll take it!" Julian cried. "And you won't be sorry, Mr. Last. No, sir, you won't be sorry."

"All right, all right," Mr. Last said, dismissing Julian with a wave of his hand. "Be here at sunup tomorrow."

Julian headed home in the dusk with the moon bobbing in the sky like a great pale melon. He jumped over low fences and let out a wild yell now and then. When he reached the rooming house, he bounded in like a young colt who'd just discovered he could run on his long, skinny legs. Julian hadn't been so happy since he was a little boy too young to know he was a slave.

"I'm an apprentice wagon maker," Julian announced at the supper table.

"Good for you," Mrs. Lawton said with a big smile.

"Four dollars a week!" Julian said.

"That's wonderful, Julian," Dinah said as she placed a plate of biscuits on the table.

"And I owe it all to you!" Julian said, standing up and sweeping her off her feet.

"Settle down," Dinah laughed. "We've got work to do after supper."

"Don't worry," Julian said, returning to his chair. "I'll be ready. I plan on helping Mr. Last write up his bills of sale someday."

Julian and Dinah had been working together every night. Dinah was a patient teacher, and Julian was an eager student. In two weeks' time he had learned to string small words together into sentences.

Secretly, Julian was working on a letter to Jim Potter. He wanted to thank Jim for helping him discover who his father was. He planned on surprising Dinah with his work. And he was going to ask her to check it over before he sent it.

A few nights later, Dinah had to work late. Mrs. Marston was ill and needed Dinah's attentions. Julian took advantage of his free time to finish his letter. Then he decided to take it over to the Marstons' house. He hoped to find Dinah alone in the kitchen so he could show her the letter.

He had never been to the Marston house before. But he went around to the back of the house and rapped on the door. No one answered. Instead, the door slid open slightly under the pressure of his hand.

"Dinah?" Julian called, putting his head in the door. The house was silent. He called again, this time more loudly. Still no answer. Maybe she's in the parlor, Julian told himself, entering the kitchen. Dinah had told him that sometimes she worked on embroidery or sewing in the parlor when Mrs. Marston was sleeping.

Julian moved slowly and silently through the house, looking for the parlor. He started down a long hallway. At the end of the hall was a small room. As Julian approached, he could see a desk and shelves filled with huge volumes of books in the room. He figured it was where Mr. Marston did his account books. He decided to look in there. Maybe Mr. Marston knew where Dinah was.

Julian peered into the doorway of the little room. "Dinah!" he said. Dinah was

Elle
pleurait
et
Mrs
Marston
mort

sitting on the floor, her back to him. When she turned around, he could see she was crying. "What's wrong?" he asked, walking toward her. Suddenly he jumped back in horror. An older man lay sprawled on the floor beside Dinah. Blood was pouring from an open wound on his head.

"Julian!" Dinah gasped. "Go! Go quickly! Mr. Marston is dead!"

"But what happened?" Julian cried.

"Just go!" Dinah screamed. "In God's name, don't argue. Just go!"

Confused, Julian turned and headed back the way he came. But as he left the house, a man Julian assumed was old Hank came around the corner.

"Who the hell are you?" Hank demanded, his voice filled with suspicion. "And what was all that screaming about?"

But Julian didn't answer. Instead, he ran through the darkness, terror clutching at his heart. Mr. Marston was dead, and Hank had seen him coming out of the house!

10 Suddenly Julian heard footsteps behind him. He turned to see Dinah approaching.

"Julian," she panted when she reached him. "There's a little shack down by the river. It's in a clump of sycamore trees. Go there and wait for word from me. It's not safe for you to stay here."

"But, Dinah, what happened?" Julian asked. "What happened to Mr. Marston?"

Dinah's eyes were wide with terror. "Just go to the shack, Julian. Hurry! I'm sending Daniel too. Feelings will be running high when they find out Mr. Marston has been murdered!"

"Murdered?" Julian cried. He grabbed Dinah by the shoulders. "Dinah, do you know what happened?" he asked one more time. He looked into her eyes. He had the feeling that she knew more than she was telling him.

Dinah put her hands on Julian's chest and gave him a push. "Just go!" she sobbed. "I'll bring word of what's happening as soon as I can."

Julian hurried down the road to the little shack Dinah had described. It was shrouded in a great clump of trees and shrubbery. He entered the empty shack and threw himself into a corner. He looked around. The shack was reminiscent of other shacks he had hidden in during his escape from the Cannon plantation. Julian put his head on his knees and tried to block out the fears that rose within him. But it was no use. Suddenly in his mind, Julian was running through swamps and woodlands. He was being chased by baying dogs. He was facing the barrel of a rifle, looking into eyes filled with hatred and greed.

I'm running again, he thought despairingly. Just like before. I'm running, and white men are after me.

How far would he have to run this time? he wondered. And how could he ever be free again? There were states like Illinois where a black man could go to escape slavery. But there were no states where he could go to escape a murder charge. No matter where he went, he would be a wanted man.

In less than an hour Daniel showed

up, his eyes wide with fear. "Julian, the sheriff was just at the boardinghouse looking for you! I heard him tell Mrs. Lawton that old Hank said you killed Mr. Marston for his gold watch. Dinah told me to come here too. She said no black man is safe in Cairo tonight."

Julian's mind was spinning with fear. He had lived long enough to know that Dinah was telling the truth. The townspeople would look for a scapegoat to blame for the murder of the respected old man. If they didn't catch Julian, they'd blame someone else. And more than likely that person would be black.

"I say we run for it," Daniel said. "Let's not wait around for them to find us."

"No," Julian said, shaking his head.

"But they'll lynch us, Julian," Daniel said.

"Dinah said she'd come," Julian replied. "We have to wait for her. She'll bring news of what's happening."

Near midnight, something rustled outside the shack. Julian sprang to his feet. He took out the pocketknife he still carried. It wasn't much, he knew, but it was all he had.

"They're coming!" Daniel cried. "They're going to lynch us!"

Julian peered through a crack by the door. It was Dinah. "Let me in," she whispered.

Once inside, she handed Julian a small sack of money. "This will be enough to get you to New England," she said. "If you go quickly you can—"

Julian reached out and grasped Dinah's shoulders firmly. He looked into her beautiful dark eyes. "Dinah, you know something, don't you?" he asked.

Dinah shook her head.

"Tell me, Dinah. Please!" Julian pleaded.

Dinah began to sob then, her shoulders heaving up and down. Julian drew her close and held her against his chest. "Shhh," he said. "It's all right. Just tell us what you saw."

"H-he said . . . h-he said he'd run my mother out of business if I said anything," Dinah cried in a hoarse whisper. "He said he had ways of c-closing the boardinghouse down and th-throwing her out on the streets."

"Who said that?" Julian demanded.

"P-Percy Marston," Dinah whispered.

"Percy Marston?" Julian said. "Mr. Marston's son?"

Dinah nodded and took a deep breath. Then she continued. "He was fighting with Mr. Marston over money again. Percy wanted his father to give him a bigger allowance. When Mr. Marston refused, he told Mr. Marston that he was being frivolous with Percy's inheritance."

"Go on," Julian said.

"I was upstairs in Mrs. Marston's bedroom. Percy didn't know I was there because I usually don't work that late. Suddenly I heard Mr. Marston cry out. I went downstairs and found Percy kneeling over his father taking the watch out of his pocket. And Mr. Marston was d-dead."

"Dinah, are you saying Percy Marston killed his father?" Julian asked.

"Yes, and he made it look like a robber did it," Dinah said, wiping her eyes with the apron she still wore.

"Dinah, you have to tell the sheriff what you saw," Julian said.

Dinah shook her head. "I can't. Percy said he'd ruin my mother. She worked so hard to get that boardinghouse, Julian. It's her whole life. I can't let him take it away from her."

Daniel spoke up now. "Dinah, even if you keep quiet, sooner or later Percy Marston is going to see you as being a danger to him," he said. "You won't be safe. Not you or your mother. He's just trying to buy time until he can figure out what to do."

"He's right, Dinah," Julian concurred.

"Julian, even if I did go to the sheriff, he wouldn't believe me," Dinah said. "It would be my word against a white man's."

Julian thought a moment. Dinah was right. Without some kind of proof, the sheriff probably wouldn't believe her. "Dinah, where do you think the gold watch is now?" he asked.

Dinah thought for a moment and said, "I think Percy still has it. He's the greediest man I know. I think he'll keep the watch and take it north with him on one of his trips. Then he'll sell it."

"Do you think the watch is somewhere in the Marston house?" Julian asked.

Dinah nodded. "I think so," she said. "It's probably in Percy's bedroom."

Julian took the girl gently in his arms. "Dinah, go to Sheriff Plummer, and tell him what you saw. Tell him you have proof that what you say is true. Then take him to the Marston house and together look for the watch."

"I can't," Dinah cried. "He's the law. He'll never believe me. He'll say I'm covering up for you or for Daniel."

"Dinah, you have to try," Julian said. "If it doesn't work, we'll run. Maybe we can make it to Canada before they catch us. But if it works, Dinah, you'll have done a great thing—for me, and for Daniel, and for all black people."

"Oh, Julian . . . I," Dinah was about to repeat that she couldn't to it, but then she whispered, "I'll try." She pulled her shawl tightly around her shoulders and started for the door. Then she paused and turned. "If I'm not back by dawn, take the money I gave you and run because you'll know I've failed."

Julian and Daniel passed a restless night. Julian drifted in and out of dreams. In one dream, slave catchers were chasing them. In the next, a lynch mob was coming after them. He finally woke just before dawn to the sound of wagon wheels approaching.

"Who is it?" Daniel whispered.

Julian peered through the crack by the door. "Sheriff Plummer. And he has Dinah with him." Julian didn't know what that meant. Did the sheriff force Dinah to lead him to them? Or had she convinced him of their innocence and he had brought her here to give them the good news? He took the knife out of his pocket.

In the growing light of dawn, Julian and Daniel watched as the sheriff jumped off the wagon. He helped Dinah down, and then he turned toward the shack, holding something high in his right hand. It was not light enough yet for Julian to make out what it was.

"Come on out of there, boys," the sheriff called.

Julian tightened his grip on the knife. Neither of them said a word.

"I say come on out of there now," the sheriff repeated. "Look at what I got here. That little cutthroat Percy Marston hid it in a slit in his feather mattress!"

Julian squinted his eyes and looked hard through the crack. Dangling from the sheriff's hand was a gold watch—Mr. Marston's watch!

Suddenly Dinah was at the door. Julian opened it wide, and she flew into his arms.

"It's over, and you're safe!" she cried. "We found the watch, and Percy admitted to killing his father. The sheriff has him in jail."

"Hallelujah!" Daniel cried, throwing his hat into the air.

Julian fairly danced Dinah to the wagon. He was so happy that the freedom he had worked so hard for had not been taken away. And he realized that again he owed his good fortune to Dinah. He decided right then and there that she'd be the girl he would marry—in a church, of course.

Percy Marston was sent to prison for

the murder of his father. His mother died soon after, and the Marston place was sold. Out of a job, Daniel went to work for Mr. Last, whose business by then was flourishing.

Julian and Dinah were married in the spring of 1859. A year later, the Civil War began—the war that would end slavery across the country. Julian and Daniel joined the Union army and served in the 54th Massachusetts Colored Infantry. This unit drew black volunteers from all over the United States. Two of Frederick Douglass's sons served in the same unit.

Daniel died in 1863 during an assault on Fort Wagner in South Carolina. Forty percent of the 54th died that day. But Julian survived the war. He returned to Cairo and took up wagon-making again. He and Dinah became the parents of two sons and three daughters—all born as free Americans who never knew the fear of losing their freedom.

Novels by Anne Schraff

PASSAGES

An Alien Spring
Bridge to the Moon (Sequel to *Maitland's Kid*)
The Darkest Secret
Don't Blame the Children
The Ghost Boy
The Haunting of Hawthorne
Maitland's Kid
Please Don't Ask Me to Love You
The Power of the Rose (Sequel to *The Haunting of Hawthorne*)
The Shadow Man
The Shining Mark (Sequel to *When a Hero Dies*)
To Slay the Dragon (Sequel to *Don't Blame the Children*)
A Song to Sing
Sparrow's Treasure
Summer of Shame (Sequel to *An Alien Spring*)
The Vandal
When a Hero Dies

PASSAGES 2000

The Boy from Planet Nowhere
Gingerbread Heart
The Hyena Laughs at Night
Just Another Name for Lonely (Sequel to *Please Don't Ask Me to Love You*)
Memories Are Forever

PASSAGES to History

Dear Mr. Kilmer
Dream Mountain
Hear That Whistle Blow
Strawberry Autumn
Winter at Wolf Crossing